P9-CFL-467

SCOOBY-DOO!™

Curse of the Lake Monster

Adapted by
Sonia Sander

Based upon the film written by
Steven Altiere & Daniel Altiere

Based on characters created by
Hanna-Barbera Productions

SCHOLASTIC INC.
New York Toronto London Auckland
Sydney Mexico City New Delhi Hong Kong

No part of this publication may be reproduced, stored in a retrieval system, or transmitted in any form or by any means, electronic, mechanical, photocopying, recording, or otherwise, without written permission of the publisher. For information regarding permission, write to Scholastic Inc., Attention: Permissions Department, 557 Broadway, New York, NY 10012.
ISBN 978-0-545-28666-4
Copyright © 2010 Hanna-Barbera.
SCOOBY-DOO and all related characters and elements are trademarks of and © Hanna-Barbera.
Published by Scholastic Inc. All rights reserved.
SCHOLASTIC and associated logos are trademarks and/or registered trademarks of Scholastic Inc.
12 11 10 9 8 7 6 5 4 3 2 1 10 11 12 13 14 15/0
Printed in the U.S.A. 40
First printing, September 2010

As soon as school let out for summer, Scooby and the gang hit the road!

They had lined up jobs at Daphne's Uncle Thorny's country club on the lake.

"Hey, get a load of that purple boat!" laughed Shaggy. "She should be called the *S.S. Daphne.*"

"Fred, where are the directions?" asked Daphne.
"Don't worry," said Fred. "We're not lost."
"Are you sure?" asked Shaggy. "Because we went by that parking lot before."
"I bet we can get some help at this gas station," said Daphne.

TROWBURG'S
GAS & GOODS
BAIT

Inside the shop, Shaggy saw a creepy photo on the wall. "Like, maybe we should just find our own way to your uncle's country club," he said.

"The country club? Don't go there! Turn back now!" warned the owner, Hilda Trowburg. "Mark my words, the Lake Monster will return!"

"You heard the lady," cried Shaggy, running out the door.

Back in the parking lot, Velma held up a flyer. “It says in here that the creature lives at the bottom of the lake.”

“Come for the view,” gulped Shaggy. “Stay for certain death!”

“It’s just a legend,” said Fred. “Let’s get going or we’ll be late.”

Uncle Thorny was very glad to see Daphne and meet her friends.

Later that day, Shaggy, Scooby, and Velma were out by the lake.

"Look at this," said Velma. "It's a rare moonstone. It glows like the moon and is said to be a magic stone."

A few minutes later, Velma started feeling sick. "I think I need to go lie down in my room."

That night, while Velma rested, the gang went to Uncle Thorny's party.

Scooby and Shaggy headed right for the food. But they didn't get to eat much before a thick fog rolled into the tent.

"Like, look at that," said Shaggy. "Who ordered the pea soup?"

But it wasn't pea soup. It was the Lake Monster, and he was not happy!

"Like, run!" cried Shaggy.

No one had a chance to get away. The monster was too fast. It knocked the whole tent down.

OLD TOWN

"It's going to be a very short summer if this mystery isn't solved," said Uncle Thorny. "That Lake Monster practically destroyed my golf course! It's full of holes!"

"Guys, we have to do something," said Daphne.

"Oh, brother," sighed Shaggy. "Here we go again."

"We should start with Elmer Uggins," said Velma. "He's the only one who's ever taken a photo of the monster."

Elmer Uggins lived in an old, spooky lighthouse. When no one answered the door, the gang split up to look for clues.

It didn't take long for the Lake Monster to find them.

Luckily, it wasn't the real Lake Monster. It was just Elmer Uggins!

"I was pretending to be the Lake Monster," he said. "So I could take pictures and sell Lake Monster postcards."

Elmer Uggins told the gang all about the Lake Monster.

"A very long time ago, Wanda Grubwort lived in a cave by the lake. One day, some new people moved to the lake. Wanda told them if they didn't leave, she would curse them. When the people stayed, she used her magic staff. She turned a frog into the Lake Monster to scare them."

Back at the golf club, the Lake Monster caught up with the gang again.

Luckily, Scooby rode in and saved Shaggy.

"Rhy'll rave roo, Raggy!" he howled.

Fred and Daphne hid in the golf shop.

The Lake Monster didn't see them.

But Fred and Daphne saw the monster — and the monster's boss!

They just couldn't see the boss's face.

Safe from the monster, the gang went to find Velma.

They found her asleep by the lake. She had warts all over her hands.

"Warts? Jinkies!" cried Velma. "What did I miss?"

"There was purple paint on the mystery boss's cloak, " said Daphne. "The same paint as on the boat Shaggy saw."

Fred and Daphne found the boat . . . and a clue.
"Looks like old newspapers," said Fred.
"It's about what happened to Wanda. Her staff was destroyed, and the magic stones were buried," read Daphne.

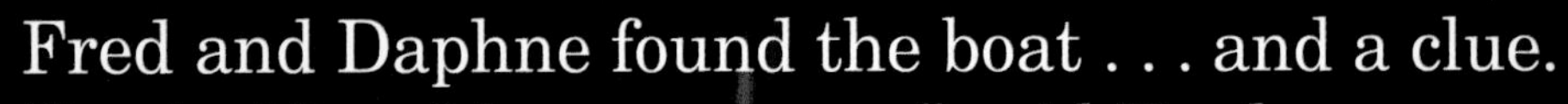

ERIE POINTE
FLOATING
MUSEUM
CLOSED
FOR RENOVATIONS

“The monster must be looking for the buried stones!” said Fred.

“Yes, but who is the monster?” asked Daphne.

“Maybe this will help us,” said Fred, holding up a paper. “Wanda had children.”

Back in Shaggy's room, Daphne looked up "Grubwort" in the phonebook.

Shaggy found a clue in an ad on the back of the book. "Hey, do you see that?" he asked, looking into the mirror. "If you spell 'Trowburg' backward, you get 'Grubwort.'"

The gang jumped into the Mystery Machine and rushed back to Trowburg's Gas and Goods.

The mystery boss was already there. The person under the hood was . . . Velma!

TROWBURG'S
GAS & GOODS

"Now that I have rebuilt my staff, no one can stop me!" cried Velma, running out the door.

"Why is Velma doing this?" asked Daphne.

"She's not herself," said Hilda Trowburg. "When Velma found that moonstone, Wanda took over her body. I bet she's gone back to her old caves."

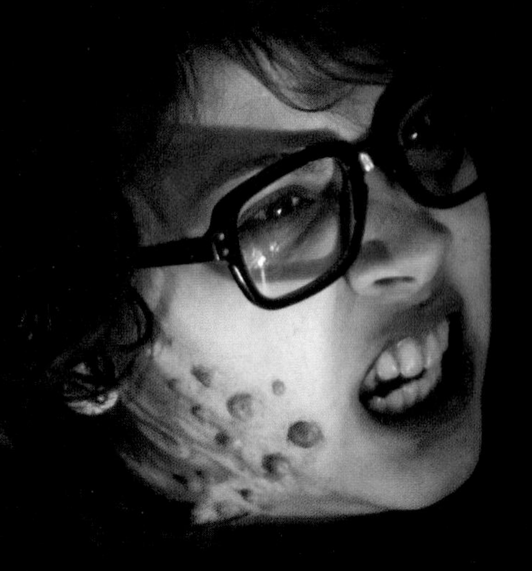

The gang raced to Wanda's old caves to save Velma.

With Shaggy and Scooby's help, Velma fought off Wanda.

"Ray rood-bye, ricked ritch!" barked Scooby, as he broke the staff.

With a burst of blue light, Wanda was gone forever.

"Is it over?" Velma asked, blinking.
"Ruh-huh," said Scooby.
"Well, gang, looks like that's another mystery solved!" Fred declared.
"Our summer vacation is saved! Come on, everyone!" cried Shaggy. "Group hug!"